Originally published in Germany in 1993 by
Ravensburger Buchverlag Otto Maier GmbH, Ravensburg,
under the title *Sie folgten einem hellen Stern.*
Text based on the poem *El Pessebre*, © 1943 Joan Alavedra

This edition published in Great Britain in 1995 by
PAVILION BOOKS LIMITED
26 Upper Ground, London SE1 9PD

A CIP catalogue record for this book is available
from the British Library.

ISBN 1 85793 756 2

Set in Aldus
Printed in Germany

2 4 6 8 10 9 7 5 3 1

This book can be ordered direct from the publisher. Please contact
the Marketing Department. But try your bookshop first.

THEY
FOLLOWED
A BRIGHT STAR

Based on a poem by JOAN ALAVEDRA

Illustrated by ULISES WENSELL

PAVILION

Long ago, on a cold and bitter night, a group of shepherds sat huddled around a fire.

"Quiet!" one of them said. "Do you hear that? Is someone singing?"

"It's only a fiddle playing in the distance," said another shepherd.

"No, it's just a lamb bleating," said a third.

Suddenly, an angel with shimmering wings appeared before them. "Arise, shepherds, and come!"

The shepherds were frightened and crouched closer around the fire.

But the voice of the angel rang out again. "A miracle will happen in Bethlehem. The Christ child will be born in a stable. Arise and come! The star will lead you!"

Then the night was still.

The shepherds looked at one another.

"What gift shall we take to the child?" asked the shepherd boy.

"We will take the finest things we have," said the oldest shepherd. "A hen, a lamb, a turkey, and a jug of honey. The dog will watch our sheep. Come!"

So they left their flock and set out to follow the bright star.

Soon the shepherds came to the top of a mountain, where a man was drawing water from a spring. "Greetings!" they said to him. "We are going to Bethlehem to see the child who will be born in a stable. Come with us!"

"I cannot," said the man. "It is I who protect the water. An angel told me that the child will need it someday."

"Very well," said the shepherds. "We wish you peace on this good night."

They walked on until they came to a riverbank. There a fisherman sat, staring deep down into the water. "Come with us," said the shepherds. "We are going to Bethlehem to see the child who will be born."

"I cannot," said the fisherman. "An angel appeared to me and said, 'Cast your line into the water and wait. He who is born will need the fish you catch. And he too will be a fisherman.'"

"The angels have been busy," said the shepherds. "We wish you peace on this good night." And they went on.

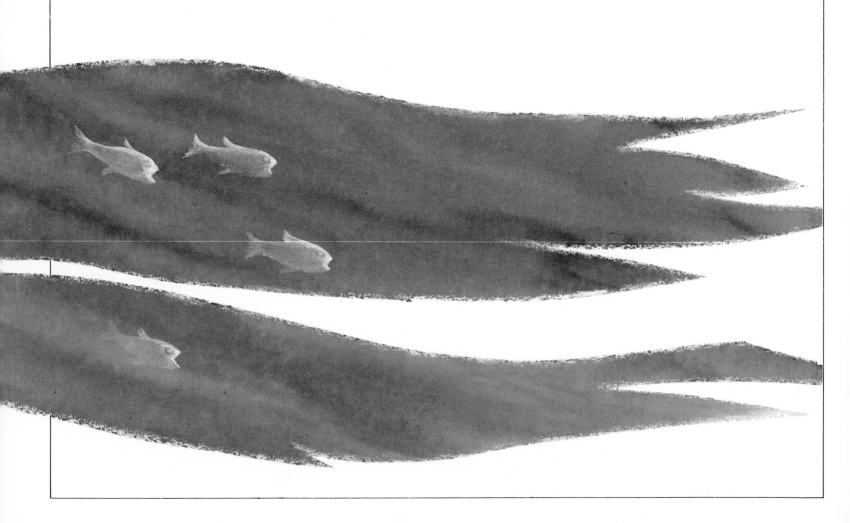

When the shepherds reached a field, they saw a man plowing.
"Hello!" the shepherds called. "Stop plowing and come with us
to see the miracle!"

"I cannot," said the plowman. "I must plow and sow, thresh the wheat,
and grind the corn to make bread with a golden crust."

"But you will have time for that later," said the shepherds.

"Oh no!" said the man. "Tonight a magnificent angel stood before my bed.
'Go and plow your field,' the angel told me. 'The child to be born will need
bread.'"

"Very well, we wish you peace on this good night," the shepherds said,
and they moved on.

The shepherds shivered with cold. At the edge of an olive grove,
they saw a man and a woman coming from their vineyard. Each of them
carried a pack full of grapes.

"Why do you harvest so late in the season?" asked the shepherds.
"Come with us to see the child who will be born."

The man pointed to his pack. "Do you see these grapes? A voice
from the heavens told us we would find new grapes in the winter fields.
And here you see them! We must make wine now, and store it until it is
needed."

"Very well," said the shepherds again. "We wish you peace on this good
night."

The little band of shepherds walked on. "This night is full of secrets," one of them wondered aloud. Above them the star still shone, its silver light filling the sky. The shepherds saw no one else for miles and miles, but they were not the only ones following the star.

Three kings were riding across the mountains, traveling over high passes and through deep valleys. Their names were Melchior, Caspar, and Balthasar, and they too had gifts for the child.

Their servants grumbled among themselves.

"I don't know if I can go any farther!" complained one.

"I wish I had a pillow to rest my head," said another.

"I wish we could stop at an inn," cried the third. "We could be sitting by the fire, eating hot soup!"

The kings looked at their maps, but their maps told them nothing. Like the shepherds, they could only follow the bright star.

"We must hurry," the kings said to one another, "for the star will disappear with the morning light."

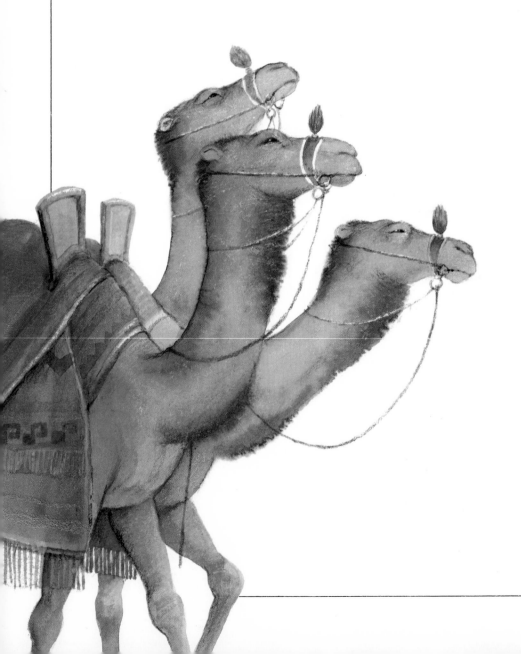

Mary and Joseph had been waiting for this night. Months before, an angel had appeared before Mary and said, "Mary, blessed are you among all women. And blessed is the child you will carry, Baby Jesus!" Mary and Joseph knew this was a gift from God.

So on that night, Mary and Joseph had settled into a stable, where the animals made room for them. And as the kings and the shepherds hurried toward the star, a radiant light filled the stable.

The animals lifted their heads at the sound of a newborn child's cry.

When the kings and the shepherds arrived, their hearts were so full that they forgot their hard journey.

"We followed the star!" the shepherd boy said.

"We come bearing gifts," said King Melchior. "Incense, myrrh, and a chest full of gold. Enough for a kingdom."

"Is the baby a king or is he a shepherd?" whispered the boy.

"Hush," the oldest shepherd told him.

"Would the child like it if I played my flute for him?" asked the shepherd boy.

So the boy played for the child and the others quietly offered their gifts to him. Then an angel appeared and said, "Kings and shepherds, rejoice! Let the world rejoice!"

And far away,
the man watched the well,

the fisherman fished,

the plowman sowed,

and the man and the woman aged the wine.

For the time would come
when Jesus would need
water and fish and bread and wine.
Water to cleanse the souls of the weary,
fish to multiply to feed the many,
and bread to break with the wine
on another night of miracles.
But on that night,
those who could not follow the star
remembered the words of the angels.

Let the world rejoice!